In Love With His Lies

By Dantwoinykue

I

Dedications

Samantha —

To my grandmother — Gone too soon!

To my father — Rest in peace Dad. I

love you so much!

Contents

Chapter One: FLIP THE SCRIPT...................................1

Chapter Two: "Perfect" Doesn't Exist.......................11

Chapter Three: Love at first sight? Bullshit...............20

Chapter Four: Payphone.......................................31

Chapter Five: Dancing in The Dark.........................38

Chapter Six: Crack in The Grass............................51

Chapter Seven: Times Like Theses.........................63

Chapter Eight: This Is How a Heart Breaks...............72

Chapter Nine: The fine art of bullshit.....................83

Chapter Ten: Expecting the Unexpected.................91

Chapter Eleven: A lot like Christmas......................99

Chapter Twelve: Someone Like You......................112

Chapter Thirteen: Our Last Chance......................123

Chapter Fourteen: Empty Words..........................133

Chapter One: FLIP THE SCRIPT

Capri waited for the groceries to come down the conveyor belt so that she could ring them up. Her feet were on fire, and she was so ready to go home. Albertsons is the last place she wanted to be on a Saturday night, and she was waiting for 11 when her shift was over. However, she wore her fake smile at the customer that was standing before her.

"It's such a lovely night, isn't it?" The little old lady asked Capri as she pulled her wallet out of her purse.

"Yes ma'am, the weather is finally starting to get cool." The Florida weather was so bipolar, but the month of November brought rain and cool weather.

Soon as Capri was done scanning all her items, Capri turned the screen to face the little old lady. "That'll be 57.90!" As the lady handed Capri the money, Capri could hear snickering from behind her. She turned around and noticed Reign, her boyfriend's baby mama, and her friends laughing from the other side of the checkout line.

Capri rolled her eyes and focused on getting the lady her change before she ended up snapping on the peasants who had just appeared in her presence. "Here you go ma'am have a lovely night."

The lady looked over Capri's shoulder then back at Capri. "You as well my dear, don't sweat the haters, if we weren't doing the right things, nobody would be hating on us."

This caught Capri off guard that the lady had caught the messy shade that came from behind her.

She couldn't help but agree and giggle at the lady, "Yeah I don't let the small stuff like that bother me."

"Good, you're too beautiful to care. Have a nice night darling." The lady grabbed her items and walked towards the door. Capri turned around to see if Reign was still standing behind her, but she was gone. Capri pulled out her phone from her apron and texted Travis to tell him that his baby mama was at her job on what she thought was some bullshit. Reign stayed on the other side of town, yet she wanted to make her presence known in her store.

Capri waited for about 10 minutes for Travis to reply but nothing came through. She slid the phone into her pocket as soon as Reign and her friends came to her line. Capri rolled her eyes and Reign giggled silently. "What's up Capri?" Reign smiled as she spoke.

Capri looked Reign up and down and grabbed the bag of chips and wine Reign had put on the conveyer belt. "ID please," Capri requested trying to keep the conversation as short as possible.

"Girl you know you don't need to card me, but I'd hate for you to lose your little day job, so I'm just going comply, here." Reign shoved the ID in Capri's face.

Capri slightly moved her head back. She punched in the numbers of Reign's birthday while trying to keep her composure. She felt her foot tapping harder under the cash register stand and she believed at any moment she was about to explode. *I'll slap this hoe in her face right now!* Capri thought to herself as she bagged up Reign's thing.

"That'll be $21.38," Capri said through gritted teeth.

"Let me dig in here and see if I got some of this good old child support money from my baby daddy." Reign and her friends laughed together. This was another dig that Capri just took for the sake of not losing her job. Reign knew not to try her outside of her job, so she thought it was funny that she wanted to come here to start with her.

She handed Reign the bag and Reign snatched it. "I think it's funny that someone who has already gotten their ass beat several times would still decide to keep trying me, Reign please stop while you're ahead."

Reign's smile dropped and she shook the bag in Capri's face while walking away. Capri laughed at the thought of that supposedly being a scare tactic. This wasn't Capri's first run-in with Travis's baby mother, and she knew it wouldn't be the last time.

One thing for sure though, she was tired of dealing with all their shit.

Capri's phone started to vibrate, and she looked around to make sure her floor supervisor wasn't walking around before she slid the phone out of her apron. Travis finally responded but as usual, it was him telling Capri to chill.

Travis: Don't even say anything to her Capri, seriously, I don't need this shit right now.

Capri rolled her eyes. *He didn't need this shit.* Capri thought as she slid the phone back down in the apron opening. She didn't need it either, yet here she was, dealing with the shit for 3 years straight. And that was just the shit she put up with from Travis. She was having to deal with Reign and the baby mama, baby daddy drama, seeing that Reign had recently given birth to Travis's baby girl.

So many people questioned Capri on her decision to stay with Travis knowing that he had openly cheated on her and now had a daughter that was shown off by the loudest person in the hood. It was always like a cheater to cheat with a bitch that was a downgrade from their woman.

Yet, Capri stood beside him. Even knowing that he had his fucked-up ways she didn't let any outside force shift her position and the title she felt like she held. Call it dumb, but Capri was in love with Travis, and it wasn't anything no one could do it about. That was her man. At least that's what she would tell herself.

A few hours passed by, and Capri was closing her station and clocking out of the store. She pulled her phone out of her pocket and check to see if Travis had called her. He knew to be at her job right at 11 because it typically didn't take that long for her to close her station. Yet here it was 11:05 pm and he still wasn't outside. Capri dialed his number, and it went straight to voicemail. "What the fuck Travis," Capri said out to nobody.

Capri went and sat on the bench outside of her store. She waved to her coworkers leaving the store. Declining a ride from a couple of them because she was wondering where in the fuck her man was. At about 11:20 loud music could be heard from the top of the empty parking lot. Soon he pulled up next to her and Capri took her time getting inside the car.

"Travis why were you late!" Capri didn't even bother getting in the car well before she started to go off on Travis. Her car was fumigated with weed smoke, and he had the music playing loud as hell. She was annoyed, to say the least. One thing she didn't like to do was wait after work, especially when she was the one with the car at the moment.

"Capri damn bae, why is it that you want to spazz all the time? Like sit back and relax." Travis tried to hand Capri the half-lit blunt in his hand, but she wasn't interested. The only thing she cared about right now is getting home and relaxing. From an already exhausting day and having to put up with his baby mama shit, she was just done for the day.

Travis pulled out of the parking lot and Capri turned the music down a touch. "Travis, I meant what I said, you need to talk to Reign before I beat her ass AGAIN. Who pops up at someone's job, unless they looking to get their ass beat? The only reason she knows where I work at is because of your ass anyways, so like I said, get that bitch in check."

"Yeah yeah, yeah, cut it with all that shit Capri, here look!" Travis put the blunt down in the middle console ashtray and reached in the back seat. He reach back up with a bouquet of red roses.

"Aw, Travis these are beautiful!" Capri grabbed the handful of roses and hugged them. "Thank you, baby!"

Travis stopped at a red light. "Come here baby," he leaned closer to Capri, and she tongued him down, even leaving a few pecks on the side of his face. "I love you, Capri!" Travis turned his attention back to the road.

"I love you too Travis!" Capri loved the gesture, but she couldn't help to think about how much he had just deflected her concerns.

Chapter Two: "Perfect" Doesn't Exist

"Capri get up baby, Jada is here." Travis shook Capri until she began to stretch from her slumber.

"What," she asked, wiping the sleep from her face.

"I said that Jada was here. I need your help making a bottle though. Reign dropped her off and didn't make any bottles like I asked her to." Travis stood there bouncing a whining Jada.

Capri analyzed how helpless Travis looked and then looked at the image of him standing there with his daughter that wasn't born by her. It hurt her at times, but she was strong, and she dealt with everything that came her way. "Travis I was on my feet all day yesterday. This is my off day. Why didn't you tell me the baby was coming?" Capri whined into the pillow.

"If I knew the baby was coming, I would've told you, babe. You know Reign be on that silly ass shit. She dropped her off early this morning."

"The fact that that hoe knows where I stay is an issue for me. I told you, you need to get baby Jada from wherever the hell yall was meeting up when yall was fucking around. She's not welcomed over here. I'm not playing."

"Damn Capri, why she gotta be all that?" Capri cut her eyes at Travis signaling for him to shut the hell up. She knew damn well he wasn't trying to correct her on speaking on a bitch he was messing around with, that just so happened to be his baby mama. "Never mind, you're right. So, are you going to make the bottle or not?"

"Damnit Travis it's not that hard." Capri pulled the covers and got up from the bed.

"Thank you!" Travis said with a hint of attitude.

"Travis, you need to come to watch me. Ain't no way you don't know how to make a bottle. Jada has been around for 6 long months. I'm going to need for you to get it together."

Capri could hear Travis mumbling from the background, however, he followed her to the kitchen. Their home that they shared wasn't much, but it was theirs. They had a 2/1 ½ townhome that they rented. Capri used the other room for her office space, but since Travis had the baby, he insisted on splitting it to make room for the baby. So, some of her things were over there for when she came to stay with them.

Capri grabbed the can of formula and held it in Travis's face. "You scoop two of these things and put it in the bottle. Then you add the water to the bottle. It's simple Travis. I think you just tried to wake me up so I can be with baby Jada and I'm not doing it. I told you I'm tired."

"I don't want you to do anything," Travis sat down at the barstool by the counter. "I just thought we could have a little family time."

"Travis since when you want to have family time. You not slick!" Capri put the bottle in the microwave for 15 seconds and shook the bottle once she took it out. "Just hand her here." Travis smiled kissed Jada on the cheek and handed her to Capri.

Capri bounced Jada as she started to get a little fussy again. "You look so good with her. You know this should've been our baby."

Capri looked at Travis with disgust. "Yea, but my man couldn't keep his dick in his pants, so now we're here."

"See here you go with this shit. Like you never want to have a good day. Always want to bring up the shit that transpired. The shit happened, Jada here, but you know damn well I don't want Reign's ass at all."

"You still were messing with that bitch behind my back, then you got some nerve to say that Jada should've been mine. That's offensive and disrespectful as hell. You know what, it's too early for this. Just get out of my face please."

Travis started to say something and decided against it. He took off out of the kitchen. Capri stared down at Jada. She was a perfect mix of her mother and father. Capri felt tears welling up, but she fought against it. "Let's get some milk in you Jada boo."

Capri would never mistreat Jada or any child for that matter based on her father's mistake. She decided to stay so she planned to care for Jada as if she was her own. As far as Reign was concerned, she could go play in traffic blindfolded and Capri wouldn't give a damn.

She'd never forget the day that Travis came through the door looking sick as a dog and pale as a ghost. She'd thought that somebody had died the way he rushed through the door slamming it and hitting the wall, leaving a hole in it.

"Travis, what in the hell happened? Why are you putting holes in the wall? Is everything okay? Somebody died?" Capri could barely get her thoughts together while pacing right alongside Travis trying to get him to use his words.

"Capri baby, I don't know how to tell you this man, I really fucked up this time." Travis rubbed his hands across his face.

"What did you do?" Capri didn't know what to think, but she just was ready for the worst.

"That bitch Reign is pregnant man, Cody just told me that bih just went to the corner screaming it to anybody that would listen."

Capri's heart dropped. "So, you mean to tell me the same bitch you swore up and down that I was delusional about, is pregnant, with your baby!" Capri threw emphasis on each word that she spoke. Before she knew it, she had slapped Travis right in the face. "I can't fucking believe you!"

"Capri, baby I don't even know if the baby is mine. Man, I know I don't deserve you, but baby don't leave me, please don't leave me. I know I fucked up but don't leave me." Travis tried to wrap his arms around Capri, but she started to swing wildly, hitting Travis in any spot that her hand would connect to.

"You are a lying son of a bitch, get the fuck out, get the fuck out of my house!" Capri's face went from anger to sadness then back to anger. Tears started to fill her eyes as she continued to swing, making sure to connect every time.

Needless to say, Capri still forgave Travis. Even after the arguments, fights with Reign, and especially when the blood test came back. Capri stood by his side. Capri walked up the stairs with the baby and laid back in the bed. She began to feed her and shortly after Travis joined them in the bed. "I didn't mean to upset you, Capri."

"Yeah, I know Travis, this whole thing is just so hard to deal with. Please just be sensitive while we get through this. Jada is only 6 months, but it's still hard."

"I understand. Now, let's watch a movie or something together, as a family." Capri cringed whenever he said the family word, but she left it alone and handed him the remote from on her side of the bed. Travis kissed both Capri and Jada on their foreheads and turned to find something on the tv. To Capri this is what she wanted her family to be, however, she wanted a child of her own.

Chapter Three: Love at first sight? Bullshit

Three Years Ago

"Capri girl hurry so that we won't miss the movie." Harmony called for Capri at the bar. They were currently at the movie theaters, but Capri needed a little liquid enhancer to make this movie worthwhile.

"Girl I'm coming, I need to get my drink first." Capri turned her body back to the bartender as she ordered her Long Island Iced Tea.

"I'm not missing the movie because of you! You always want to drink."

"Girl and you always being a party pooper. I'm sure the previews are playing. I don't need you to stay out here with me, I'm a big girl. You can go in there with London. Can you take my popcorn though?" Capri handed her popcorn to Harmony. Harmony headed to the theater and Capri waited for the bartender to finish mixing her drink. She wanted to make sure her drink was strong and good, so she requested the bartender put more than a double shot in her drink.

"Yo shorty let me buy you a drink," a dude came up behind Capri and put his hand on her shoulder.

"Sir don't touch me, I don't even know you like that," Capri said with a quickness. She hadn't even gotten a chance to see who had touched her without permission. When she turned around, she couldn't help but drool over this handsome tall caramel-skinned man who seemed to have a respectful feel about him.

He had muscular arms that were covered in tattoos and large hands, Capri looked down and noticed his tone legs. *Damn,* she thought as she connected back to his eyes. He had a smile of a charmer and somehow, she had a feeling she wasn't going to be able to resist whatever it is he was offering.

"So, what's up you gone let me buy you a drink?"

"Again, I don't know you like that. Why you wanna buy me a drink?" Capri asked but more so was flirting with this unknown gentleman.

"Damn ma, it's just a drink. No foul, no harm, just a drink baby girl."

The bartender had come over with her drink as the mystery man was waiting for her reply. "That'll be $13.50, ma'am."

The dude began to pull out some money before Capri had a chance to provide her answer. "Thank you, man, keep the change."

Capri grabbed a napkin and wrapped it around her drink. "Thank you, stranger," she stated jokingly.

"Ouch, you just out to get me tonight aren't you. My name is Travis. Travis Jackson, but my friends call me Trav. I noticed you and your homegirls when yall walked in the mall then again here at the movies. I thought I'd be a fool to pass up my opportunity to say something to you, but you are so damn feisty I think I've changed my mind." Travis said now, joking himself.

"You can't just be touching people you don't know." Capri looked down at her ticket to see which theatre she was in.

"What you came here to see?"

"Jason Vs Michael Myers."

"Well would you look at that, so am I," Travis sang holding up his movie ticket.

"So, what does that mean?" Capri headed in the direction of her theatre while taking a sip out of her cup.

"That means, can a brother watch the movie with you?"

"You said you saw me here with my girlfriends, why would you think we need a third wheel?" Capri was giggling so hard at this point.

"Yo, what's so funny man? I'm simply going to sit around the area where you and your girls are sitting. It's just a movie. Come on what's the issue?"

Capri looked down at her watch and now she hurried along to get to the movies. "Look if you're coming come on. You're holding me up." Capri allowed Travis to follow behind her as she made her way into the theater. She spotted her friends and climbed the stairs to sit with them, Travis was right on her heels.

She took a seat right next to her friends and Travis took the seat next to her. Capri's friends looked over at the stranger and then their friend. Capri smiled and threw up her hand waving them off. Right now, she didn't feel like explaining to them how this stranger ended up inserting himself in girl's night but at this point, she just wanted to enjoy the movie.

As soon as the movie ended, and the theatre lights came on Harmony and London both looked over at Travis. "Now Capri, who is this man?" Harmony questioned while keeping her eyes fixated on Travis.

"My name is Travis. I meant no harm intruding, I just had to enjoy a night out with y'all's mean friend."

"Mean?" Capri asked.

"You got that right," London interjected.

"Excuse me," Capri faked rolled her eyes.

The crew all stood up and made their way out of the theatre. "So, who are you, sir?" Harmony asked as Travis held the door open for all of them.

"I'm Travis!" Capri couldn't help but notice

how charming he was even while about to get grilled

by both of her friends.

"Well, I got that the first time, Travis, how'd

you end up with us? How do you know Capri?"

"Capri is her name huh?" Travis looked over

at Capri and she blushed. "Well, I don't know her yet.

But I couldn't help but notice her and I just had to get

her attention. She was throwing daggers at your boy

though. What's up with that?"

"No, I wasn't!" Capri laughed. "I was simply

trying to figure out why as stranger touched my

shoulder. That's all."

"Well, that's the thing, I'm not trying to be a

stranger, not for long. You gone give me your

number and a chance to get to know you a little

more?" Travis felt confident that he would be getting

Capri's number that night. He pulled his phone out and moved it close to Capri.

"Girl, give that man your number. You know you ain't had a man in ages," London giggled.

Harmony moved his phone back slightly, "wait a damn second, you're not a serial killer or stalker, are you? Cause my girl ain't getting mixed up in some bullshit!" Harmony said in a serious tone.

"Harmony!" Capri shrieked.

Travis held his hands up, "I have nothing but good intentions with your friend I promise!"

"Well good, Capri hurry up and give him your number so we can go girl. We got shit to do." Harmony pushed Capri closer to Travis.

Travis grabbed Capri up gently by the waist. "So pretty girl, are you going to give a brother your number?"

"Give me your phone." Capri held her hand out waiting for Travis to unlock his phone and hand it to her.

"Yo Trav, where the hell did you go bro? I just watched this whole movie without you." Just as Capri was typing in her phone number a man came from the entrance of the mall. Capri thought this must have been Travis's friend. She knew that he couldn't have come to the movies alone, but seeing his friend made sense.

"Here's my number. Don't be acting all weird now!" Capri joked.

"I got you. Girl, you don't even know it yet, but you will be my wife."

"See here go the weird shit. Let me delete my number," Capri laughed while reaching for the phone.

"Too late now," Travis slid the phone in his pocket. "I'll catch you later shorty."

"See you later Travis," Capri said joining her friends.

Chapter Four: Payphone

It was midday and Capri woke up from her nap. Both Travis and Jada were knocked out. Capri carefully moved out of the bed making sure not to wake Jada up in the process. Jada was a pretty good baby, so Capri had no trouble out of her whenever she came over. Travis started to snore so Capri, quietly but quickly removed herself from the room.

She grabbed the blanket that hung over the couch and weirdly, as it unfolded, Travis's cellphone came rolling out of it. "What the hell?" Capri bent down to grab it and continued to the couch to lay down. As she cut the tv on she placed the phone on the armrest.

As she got into her show, she couldn't help but notice Travis's phone kept vibrating. She picked it up off the arm of the couch and entered in his password. After the incident with Reign, there were no secrets between the two. So that meant to get Capri back, she demanded that he come up off the password for his phone.

As she opened it, she scrolled through the notifications window and his boys were texting him in their little group chat trying to see what he was getting into tonight. It was a lot of back and forth and she laughed at some of the things they were saying to each other. Capri was about to put the phone down, but a notification came in from Reign.

Reign: Baby daddy when you drop baby girl off can we fuck one more time. That dick was good as hell that last time.

Capri's blood started to boil at the thought of Travis giving himself to Reign. All this time since the baby had been conceived, she thought that he and she were a thing in the past. For his sake, Capri hope that this bitch was lying because she was seeing red.

Seeing that prompted her to go into his text messages. Capri skimmed past all the messages she felt were not related to her mission at the moment. He had an old message on his phone from someone named Brittany. When Capri opened the text thread her eyes were blinded by the pictures of naked bodies, while some were in lingerie, most were naked pictures of this same girl.

Capri scrolled up on the message thread and noticed that there was a video sent to Travis from this same girl. When Capri clicked play her jaw dropped. There Travis was having sex with this girl. Capri watched in detail as the girl maneuvered the phone around catching Travis at every angle she could.

Capri jumped up and stormed into the bedroom throwing the phone at Travis making sure it didn't hit Jada in the process. Travis popped up from his slumber. "Yo what the fuck Capri!"

"What the fuck is right, who the fuck is that bitch in your phone Travis? I'm so sick of this shit. You just can't keep your dick in your pants, can you?"

"Capri you," Travis looked down at his phone before finishing his statement, "Capri damn this shit is old!"

"So that's the best lie you could think of?" Capri tried her best to keep her voice down. "You lucky Jada here or I would show out on your ass for real! If you want to be a hoe, go fuck with them hoes." Capri pulled some sweats out of a basket and put them on. She grabbed her purse and her keys from the dresser.

"Where are you going, Capri?" Now Travis was getting up out of the bed trying his best to try and stop Capri from leaving.

"Travis I'm getting the fuck out this house before I kill you. I don't have time for you lying ass. I'm not stupid. Get the fuck out my way before I cut up!" Capri pushed Travis who attempted to stand in the doorway of the bedroom.

"I'm not moving until you talk to me!" Travis said sternly.

"Boy get your lying cheating ass out my damn face I'm not playing with you!" This time Capri yelled causing Jada to stir in her sleep and start crying. Travis shook his head and moved out of Capri's way. "Thank you!" She made sure to slam the bedroom door on her way out of it. She started her car and used her phone to call up Harmony. She didn't feel like hearing the I told you so's from her, but she didn't have anywhere to go.

"What's up Capri," Harmony yawned into the phone.

"Harmony, I need to come over for a little while." Capri's voice was shaky, and Harmony could tell.

"What this nigga did now? Girl I'm sick of his shit for you. Every other week you're on my line crying and it doesn't be behind nobody but Travis, so what the hell he did?"

"I caught him cheating again," Capri wiped the tears that had fallen off her face.

"How many more times will you allow this nigga to cheat on you? Child, well I guess it is true what they say, only *you* know when you've had enough."

Capri started to regret calling her but now she was the only one that she could call on at the moment. She knew her friend only spoke the truth, but it was some shit that she didn't want to hear at the moment. "Harmony look, I get it, but I just don't want to hear the shit right now okay. I swear I get it."

"I'm only saying this shit because I love you. Otherwise, I'd be playing the fool with you and I'm not about to do that, but I'm home. I'll see you when you get here." Harmony disconnected the phone without saying bye and Capri continued her way.

Travis tried his best to hit up Capri's line, but she did everything but block him to ignore his calls. She was sick of his shit. Every time she felt like ending it, here he came with his lies and the apologies. Harmony was right. Only she would know when she had enough, but somewhere deep down inside of Capri she prayed her man would get it together.

Chapter Five: Dancing in The Dark

"I mean what you're telling me sounds like you already know what the hell went on." Harmony said pouring wine into the glasses.

"His ass wanna try and play me like I don't know that was some recent shit. Like where the hell does he even find the time? Like you already had a damn baby on me. You would think you'd get your shit together."

"It's the baby for me. That would've been had his ass put out. Don't get me wrong. I love you guys together, but he has some fucked up ways girl." Harmony shook her head. "You are my girl though so you're mad at him, I'm mad at him. Y'all straight, he straight, but you need to evaluate yourself and this relationship."

Capri looked down at her phone to see that Travis was still blowing her up. What was an apology turned more into angry threats of '*bringing her ass home*' so they could talk! Capri wasn't having it. She turned her phone off and took a sip of the wine Harmony had prepared them.

"This is what we need to do, we need to go out tonight!"

"Harmony you know I don't like going out like that."

"Yeah, but you need to get out that house. Hell, you are always cooped up doing motherly duties to a child that's not yours or working. We are going out tonight bitch. So do whatever it is you need to do to get out of the house. Cause I'm coming to get you!"

"Why I feel like you're up to no good."

"Girl, wait until London gets off. We about to have ourselves a good old-fashioned girl's night!" Harmony got excited and started clapping her hands and doing a little sit-down twerk on the couch.

"Yup this is a setup!"

"Oh, stop acting like an old hag. Your nigga be doing him all the time. Girl it is time for you to do you for a night. If only for one night only, this is your night sister girl!"

Capri looked at Harmony reluctantly and took another sip of her wine. "Okay Harmony, but we better not be going to one of them broke down ass clubs."

"Don't even worry about it. I'm taking your ass to the strip club!"

"The what?"

"You heard me. I'm taking you to the strip club. I don't have time for niggas to be all in our face so we going to have a good time and look at some ass and titties!" Harmony was bisexual and she always got approached by both sexes. So, this was going to be a good time for her.

Capri didn't care for the strip club either, but it was best being in the middle of a nightclub where it seemed like the niggas came to prey on their next one-night stand with a stripper instead of her, so she wasn't going to fight Harmony too much on the idea. "Fine, fine, I'll go. You're right I probably do need a night out."

"Exactly. Hell, you don't even need to go home. I got everything that you need over here. Put that nigga on ice for the night!"

Capri gave Harmony the side-eye. Now she felt like she was getting set up. She was all for going out, but not without at least communicating with Travis after their argument was a bit much for her. "I don't know about that now Harmony. You trying to start a war for real."

"His cheating ass," Harmony stopped herself. "You know what, you right, I'm going to let you handle that, but what I'm saying to you is, if you keep running back every time he fucks up. He gone keep fucking up. Trust me. I know!" Harmony got up and disappeared into the room for a little bit.

When she returned Capri was pulling out her phone to at least send Travis a message. She wasn't going to go home, but she wanted him to at least know that so he wouldn't worry and tear down the streets looking for her. "So, I texted him, so he at least knows I'm not coming back today," Cari muttered.

Harmony clapped her hands and poured more wine. "Girl's night!" She said with much excitement.

Harmony and Capri drank more wine and the both of them passed out on the couch. After a couple of hours, they both were awakened by knocks at the door. "Damn somebody knocking like the police!" Capri said holding her head. The wine had started to give her a slight headache.

"Whoooo is it?" Harmony sung.

"Bitch it's the one and only London, open the muthafuckin' door!" London was ghetto as hell for a white girl, but she always held her own.

Harmony swung the door open, "Girl don't be knocking on my door like you the police. Look at you, looking like fresh off work. Smelling like fries and shit." Harmony started to laugh.

"Bitch fuck you, I work hard for all my little coins, okay! Anyways this day ain't even about me." London pushed past Harmony. "Capri, why they fuck can't this man keep his dick in his pants, like what's up? You need me to call my brother to fuck him up?"

London's brother was in the Army, and she always was auctioning him off to beat somebody's ass. He probably didn't even know the amount of shit he was put in by his sister. "No London, I will work all that out. As of now, I'm just trying to make the best of this girl's night. I can't lie I need it. Afterward, I will deal with his lying ass."

"I know that's right," London said as she put her bags down in front of her and sat on the couch. "So, what's the plan for the night?"

"So, I was thinking the strip club. We can go to Dolla's joint, the Paradise Place."

"Oh, I heard about that spot. We gone be turnt tonight." London started snapping her fingers. Capri was the only one still reluctant to go, however, after a few more drinks and a wardrobe change, Harmony, London, and Capri all were out of the door and walking through the door of Paradise Place.

Capri felt so out of place seeing that she hadn't been to an actual club in a while. Plus, she didn't have her clothes on tonight, so she just felt so underdressed, and all her curves were falling out of the two-piece outfit Harmony let her borrow.

"This club is so dope. My homegirl owns this spot. Dolla should be somewhere around here. I'll be back." Harmony left London and Capri by the bar as she went to go find Dolla. London and Capri bobbed their heads to the music and scanned the environment.

"Damn girl, you are looking right!" Some random man walked up on Capri, damn near pressing his hard-on against her hip.

"Sir, can you please, move the hell out of my way."

"Damn lil' baby, you gone do a brother like that?" The man said looking offended.

"Dawg she not fucking with you she's married, get the hell on." London pushed the guy back away from Capri.

"I don't see no ring on this bitch's finger and who are you? Her spokesperson?" The man was drunk, and the girls were over it at this point.

"Yo bro they said to move the hell on. You on that goofy shit. All night you have been in a bitch face. Get yo old ass on!" Some man at the bar had seemingly come to their rescue.

"I'm not worried about cookies and cream no way. Plenty of other bitches in here." With that, the older man grabbed his drink off the counter and continued making his way around the club.

"Thank you for that, some people are certified weirdos," Capri stated to the guy.

"No problem Ma, I got sisters, so I know how that shit goes. Yall enjoy yall selves." The unknown guy grabbed his bottle and headed over to a section that was full of people.

"Damn that man was fine," London said in Capri's ear. Capri looked at the guy and thought about how fine he was. London wasn't exaggerating like she normally did when it came to black men. She thought almost every black man was fine, and that was certainly not the case for most.

Once Harmony came back over, she had with her, who the ladies assumed was Dolla. "Look ladies, I have yall set up in a nice little spot by the DJ booth. Feel free to enjoy complimentary drinks on me. I also am sending some of the best ladies over for your enjoyment. Harmony is there anything else I can do for your fine ass?" Dolla smiled in Harmony's direction.

"That's it, baby, I surely appreciate it." Harmony flirted back.

Dolla nodded her head and disappeared. We headed over to the booth that was getting put together for us. Capri couldn't help but randomly stare at the gentlemen that had helped her and her friend get out of the old man's web just a few minutes ago.

The whole night seemed to move at such a fast pace. With her and her girls enjoying themselves. Capri and mister man locked eyes every chance they got, and not once was Travis on her mind. That was until he slid through the door with his homeboy Cody and Keymoni.

Chapter Six: Crack in The Glass

Capri sat down in the booth trying to turn away from the crowd. Just her luck that her man would show up to the same hole in the wall club as her. "Capri why are you sitting down. Girl, that's not why I brought you here!" Harmony yelled in Capri's ear.

"Girl Travis just walked through that damn door!"

"Travis," Harmony scanned the room in disbelief.

"See every time, every time I try to have a good night, it never fails." Capri started to pout.

"Girl if you don't get up and shake some ass. Fuck him. You see where he at. If I fucked up, I'd be hounding my girl the fuck down. He's exactly where he wants to be and so are we. Get your ass up!" London pulled her friend out of the booth seat and started dancing with her.

Capri did her best to let her guard down, but she couldn't help but think at any moment Travis was going to be in her space. Just then as she scanned the room, the man from earlier at the bar came over with a drink in his hand. "Hey Miss, this is for you!"

Capri looked at the drink with her face twisted. "Um, thank you but I don't take drinks from strangers."

"Ma, I promise you I didn't do nothing to this drink but bring it over to you. I don't even plan on staying. I just saw you seeing me, and I just wanted to offer a nice gesture." The man smiled and tried to hand Capri the drink again.

Capri reluctantly took the drink and looked at the bottom of it. The man started to laugh. "Damn man, not so trusting, are we?"

"Hell, I gotta check. Ain't no telling these days." Capri took a larger gulp out of her cup.

"I don't blame you ma, well enjoy your night." The unknown man walked away.

"Damn that's a sexy ass man, and he's all over you!" Harmony was in awe.

"You know I don't be worried about that. Let's turn up!" Capri tried her best to deflect the conversation from what her friend was trying to make it. All night the girls turned up in their booth. Harmony had brought over five hundred dollars in ones. She handed one stack to each of the girls and put the rest in the middle of the table.

A few strippers that were working the floor came over to the women at the booth. One of the strippers gently pushed Capri back on the booth chair. The stripper started shaking her ass in front of Capri. Capri couldn't help but notice how the stripper's ass moved like waves in an ocean, she was mesmerized. Harmony and London gathered around Capri and the stripper and started throwing ones.

The DJ must have peeped how turnt the girls were becoming because over the mic he started screaming, "Fuck it up Aspen, they don't know how to handle all that ass. Finish her!"

Once the DJ said that Aspen got on her head and started popping pussy and ass all in Capri's face. The club went wild as Aspen contorted her body so heavenly yet sexy for Capri. She was so in tuned she'd forgotten to start throwing her money until London nudged her and pointed to her stack. Capri picked up the money and joined her girls in making it rain. The club lights started to shine on and off them as their section became lit!

Capri couldn't lie, she was loving this attention! So much, that shit didn't even notice Travis and his homeboys staring at her from a distance. As much as Travis wanted to step in and snatch her the hell up for ignoring him, he didn't want to risk having so much attention on them.

However, the second she finished this little making it rain session he was planning on marching right up on her and figuring out what the hell she had going on. He looked over at his woman who was smiling and seemed so happy. He didn't know why he kept fucking up, but he knew he didn't want to lose her. He couldn't even explain it, but he knew he needed to make a change, or he would lose Capri forever.

Aspen got back on her feet and started to pull her money into a pile. She turned back and kissed Capri on the cheek. Capri smiled and went to grab her drink. "Girl this is too much!" She shouted over to Harmony who was enjoying a lap dance herself.

"Shit this ain't *enough*!" Harmony yelled in a turnt up tone, matching the stripper's movements as she was grinding against her.

London laughed then poured more liquor into everyone's cup. Tonight, was turning out to be everything Capri didn't know she needed. After a few cups, she was feeling good and finally decided to let her hair down and join her friends in turning up.

They danced with each other, around each other, and kept popping bottles all night.

It was when Travis and his homeboys rolled up on them with the meanest mug on their faces. Harmony stood in front of Travis as she did the first time, they all met. Travis looked at her like she'd better move her ass out his way. Harmony rolled her eyes, but Capri touched her shoulder letting her know it was okay. Harmony stepped aside.

"So, this why you ain't answering a nigga's calls? You out here dressed in nothing showing your ass?" Travis had a mug on his face, but he wanted to grab her and hold her.

"Travis please don't try to flip the script. You know why I been gone all damn day. So did you fuck Reign when you dropped Jada off tonight?"

"Chill the fuck out with that." Travis grabbed her arm, but Capri quickly snatched it away.

"Don't touch me, Travis. I've had enough and I just want to enjoy my girls for the night. That's all. The strip club ain't the place for our business. We'll talk later."

As soon as Capri turned away, the dude who bought her a drink earlier had rolled up, by himself to the group. "Yo, you, okay?" He gently tugged on Capri's forearm and asked her.

Capri's eyes got big and instantly knew some shit was about to pop off. "Yo, my nigga do you know her?" Travis said almost as loud as the music was.

"Nigga my name is Mahlik, not nigga, and no I don't but do you know her? I see you over here grabbing on her and shit. Nigga it's plenty of other females in here. She looks uninterested."

"This here is my girl partna' I suggest you move the fuck around before something happen to yo ass!" Travis spat, sizing Mahlik as he spoke.

Mahlik slightly let go of Capri's arm, but he didn't move from her side. Capri rolled her eyes and spoke. "This is my boyfriend. I appreciate you checking the temperature cause niggas have been trying it all night, but that one there belongs to me."

Travis looked at Mahlik like he wanted to say, 'Told ya so', but he just stood there instead, trying to peep the next move.

"Alright Ma, I just was checking. You girls enjoy your night," he lifted his hand to the ladies. As he walked past Travis, he quickly changed his mug and started to grill him. "*Partna'*!" Mahlik spoke

once more.

"Bitch ass nigga!"

"The fuck you call me?" Mahlik doubled

back and now this time he was in Travis's face.

Travis didn't want to look lame, especially with

Capri saying she appreciated something a nigga who

wasn't him did for her.

"Bitch you heard me," was the last thing

Travis could say before the fight broke out. Travis

curled his fist up and aimed right for Mahlik's nose.

When it connected with the bridge of Mahlik's nose

he didn't even flinch. Blood trickled down but

Mahlik wasn't having it. He started to wildly swing

on Travis and they both countered each other's

punches.

It wasn't too long before Travis's friends started to pull Mahlik down and took turns stomping him in the stomach and legs. Mahlik didn't even try to guard his head. He did his best to fight and get up so that he could fuck all three of them up. However, by that time the bodyguards from the nightclub had started to pick up and escort Travis and his posse out of the strip joint. The whole-time security was dragging Travis out he was screaming for his woman. "Capri, get your ass out here. You better not stay up in this bitch. Fuck yall I don't need to be in this po' ass club!" His words grew silent over the music and then they vanished.

Capri attempted to help the man up off the ground, but he threw her hand off his and grunted at her. He got up and left out the same door her man got carried out of.

"What a fucking night!" Capri said to herself.

Chapter Seven: Times Like These

It had been two days since the fight and Travis hadn't spoken to Capri. Capri didn't care that much but it was starting to get played out that he was upset about the fact that he got kicked out of the club. She finally was making him sit down and figure out how he could beat her mad over the club incident, yet still hadn't discussed what was discovered.

"Do you know this nigga or something?" Travis had asked when Capri requested that they talk.

"Travis, what niggas I know like that? Like please come on. Like I already told you when we spoke that night, some old ass dude was trying to talk to me and London, except he was being aggressive.

So out of know where Mahlik came and told the dude

to bounce. No pressure. He didn't even try me or

anything."

"That don't make no sense. Ain't no nigga

finna just come to a bitch rescue unless he knows

her."

"First of all, I ain't no bitch. Secondly, I told

you I don't know this man. I'm not saying it again.

You and your friends wrong as hell how yall did that

man in the club."

"Oh well, shouldn't have been on that player-

type shit. Don't ever fucking play with me again

Capri. Talking about what you appreciate. I like to

knock you upside your damn head too."

"I wish the hell you would, and since we are

talking about knocking people out, let's not forget the

fact that you were cheating on me with two fucking

people. Hell, it could be more. The fact that you

cheated on me with some bitch named Brittany, okay,

I see what you did there, new pussy. But you cheat

on me with that bitch ass baby mama of yours and

think that's just supposed to be cool!"

"I didn't cheat on you Capri damn! That bitch

Brittany wasn't even sending that shit to me. I let

Keymoni use my phone and I guess he forgot to

delete that shit out my phone."

"See now you want to sit up here and lie to

my damn face. How the fuck old are we? Ain't no

nigga using the next nigga's phone to receive nudes

from a bitch. Quit fucking playing with me before I

get heated." Capri stood up out of the couch.

"Man, I'm telling you the truth. That shit with

Reign was some bullshit too baby." Capri got more

heated. It was rare that Travis called Capri baby, but

when he did, she knew that whatever came before or after that was a damn lie.

"I don't want to hear the shit, Travis. You are a gotdamn liar and a cheater. I'm so sick of your shit." Capri stormed up to the room and slammed the door behind her. Capri decided to start the shower water seeing that she had just got off work. Every time Travis got into some shit with a bitch, Capri was always given the short end of the stick.

"I'm so tired of this shit," Capri sobbed in the shower. The thought of knowing that another person had access to her man in the same sexual way had her devastated. She was so hurt in ways that she didn't think that Travis understood. Capri let the water fall onto her face. Why was this shit so hard?

She heard the bathroom door open, and she quickly held her tears and sniffles. She wouldn't dare let Travis see her broken anymore. She felt like the more she accepted the shit he brought to their doorstep the more he thought it was okay to fuck around. Capri had never cheated on him, but sometimes she wish she had the willpower to entertain another man long enough for Travis to see how the hell it felt to be broken down.

She knew if she ever cheated, Travis would have a damn heart attack. Men can't take the same hurt they dish out and Capri knew this to be all facts. "Baby, listen, that shit with Reign was a damn slip up. You know I don't even fuck with that hoe like that. She my baby moms, but only cause of a technicality."

"Technically you gave the bitch raw dick. Then came and laid up with me every night after."

Capri was now steaming more than the shower was at this point.

"See, I'm not about to get into how the shit even became a thing. I fucked up again. I know it, but damn man. Damn!"

"Yeah, damn is right. You ain't no damn good!"

"Imma let you cool off."

"Yeah, you fucking do that!" Capri tried to stay strong and hold back the tears before Travis got the satisfaction of hearing her cry.

Travis slammed the bathroom door and Capri's eyes were welded up with more tears. She wiped them violently and tried to tell herself not to cry over this or him. Capri got out of the shower and got dressed for work. Capri didn't enjoy working in the grocery store, but it got the bills paid.

She grabbed her keys and purse off the dresser and made her way out the door. Travis had already left, and she was grateful for it. She didn't want to have to deal with him right now. Capri was hoping that work would clear her mind for the day, and she would be in better spirits before the night was over.

When Capri pulled up to the job it seemed to be busier than normal, and she figured because Christmas was coming up people were trying to prepare for the holiday cooking. Capri dragged her feet going inside the store. She walked to the back office to clock in.

"Good morning, Capri, What a lovely morning." Denise, the store manager, said with a jolt of energy.

"Good morning, Denise, trying to get there!" Capri thought about her morning, and it wasn't that lovely. "What lane do you need me on today?"

"I was thinking the 10 items or less lane. You move pretty quickly, and we have been having a big pile up because of this whole Christmas shopping thing."

"You know I don't have a problem with that." Capri grabbed her apron and put it over her head. Capri went to the check-out line and cut her light on to let customers know that she was available. Soon customers started to flood her line with last-minute things that they needed.

With Christmas less than two weeks away, Capri started to think how she hadn't even begun to start on Christmas plans. Her and Travis having issues now didn't help her thoughts. She wondered what Christmas would look like this year. Would

Travis try to split time to spend with his child?

Would his family try to bring up the whole cheating

thing during Christmas? Everything was up in the air.

This was going to be the first Christmas where Travis

had other obligations and Capri didn't know how to

feel about that. She hoped that this Christmas wasn't

a complete failure.

Chapter Eight: This Is How a Heart Breaks

The day seemed to be going too well. Capri and Travis were finally back in each other's good graces. That's how things became with them. Like clockwork, they would be mad at each other, then in the next breath, one of them would be apologizing for all the drama one of them caused for the other.

Today was a regular day and there was only a week left until Christmas. Capri started putting up decorations around the house while Travis was coming down the stairs.

"You headed out baby?" Capri wondered as she climbed up the step ladder.

"Yeah, about to go meet Keymoni and Cody." Travis hadn't looked up at her yet as he was occupied by his phone.

"Travis you were supposed to help me finish up the decorations and wrap these presents for your parent's house."

"Capri that's not super important at this moment." Travis was still indulged in his phone that he had yet to look up. Capri threw a candy cane at his head, barely missing. "Yo what the hell Capri!"

"Focus. You haven't even looked up from your phone since you came in here. Like you sure you are going with Keymoni and Cody?"

Now Travis looked up from his phone, however, the look on his face showed he was now annoyed. "The hell do you mean am I sure? That's what I just told you right?" Travis huffed.

"Whatever Travis!" Capri didn't even feel like getting into it, but something told her he was about to get into some mess. She just didn't know what.

"Nah, whatever Capri, yo ass is stressful!"

"Oh, I'm the stressful one. That's new, usually, that's your role!" Capri stepped down off the ladder.

Travis huffed loudly then made his way out the door without another word to Capri. She couldn't help but wonder if he was going to see the Brittany chick or his baby moms. Either way, she knew he was up to no good. Capri went upstairs to the office and grabbed Travis's MacBook.

She sat the computer on the desk and sat in the rolling chair. For a minute she just stared at her laptop, remembering the saying, 'if you go looking for something, 9 times out of 10, you'll find something.' However, something deep down in her spirit told her to open the laptop and look at this man's messages. Capri didn't like to pry but this is what her world had somewhat turned into. Not believing a word Travis had to say.

Capri slowly opened the laptop and after entering the password messages started popping up on the side of the computer screen. She clicked the blue icon on the bottom of the screen. Capri indeed saw the group chat with Travis and his boys and after further review, he was heading to them.

Yet Capri's wondering eye and women's intuition didn't allow her to stop there. Again, there was a text from this Brittany girl. She'd been blowing Travis up for days according to the message thread. It wasn't until yesterday when he'd finally given in and texted her back, because there was a message from the girl being desperate.

Brittany: Daddy can I please have it one more time before you do that?"

Capri's insides started to boil. "This lying ass nigga!" Capri slammed the laptop down and stormed out of the office. Why couldn't he fly straight? How come from all the bullshit he still decided to cause her so much pain. These are the questions that she asked herself.

Her first thought was to get in her car and go to where he was and blow the hell up. However, she decided to play the game smarter than that. She went back to the laptop and got the chick's number and entered it into her phone. It took a couple of rings, but the girl finally answered.

"Hello?" A voice sleepily said into the phone.

"Hello is this, Brittany?" Capri said with much attitude.

"Um yeah, who the fuck is this?" Brittany sounded wide awake now.

"Why the fuck you keep hounding my nigga? Yo hoe ass can't find your own you got to fuck on somebody else's?" Capri was fuming at this point.

"Well bitch first off start by telling me who your man is," Brittany laughed into the phone. "Then we can continue with the insults."

"Bitch you such a hoe you don't even know who you be fucking with. Travis bitch. And if I catch you texting him again, imma find out where your hoe ass is at and beat your ass."

"Oh, you talking about *daddy*? He likes when I call him that. You're mad about community dick. Girl, I guess it's true what they say. Them for lifers be in it till the wheels fall off. You a miserable ass bitch. Get the fuck off my line."

"I'll beat yo ass bruh!"

"Come beat it then. Yo nigga know where I stay. Trust me!" Brittany disconnected the line.

Capri wanted to scream she was so pissed off. She called both London and Harmony on FaceTime. London was the first to pick up.

"What's up chick?" London looked like she was in her car.

"This muthafucka keep trying me. I could burn up all his shit right now!"

"Whoa wait, what are we talking about here?"

"Travis goofy ass, fucking around with some Brittany bitch. I just got off the phone with this hoe. I swear I want to pull up on this bitch."

"Shit if you got the addy we can do a little drive-by!" Capri loved that about her friends. Always down for her no matter what.

"I feel like I'm going to go to jail if I do that. Especially with all this built-up pressure."

Harmony was just joining the two on FaceTime and she looked as if she was working out. "Jail? What the hell I missed?" Harmony wiped the sweat from her face.

"Some hoe Travis fucking with. I'm just trying to see if we are pulling up!" London answered before Capri had a chance.

"Capri, we are getting too old for this. Leave this nigga alone. I'm telling you this because I love you. Stop stressing yourself out over someone who doesn't want to change."

"Girl, fuck him. Everybody knows in all of Florida who Travis belongs to. These hoes are just disrespectful as hell and sometimes you got to break a bitch down and make the whole world see not to fuck with you." London explained.

"That's some stupid shit honestly. A man gone do only what he wants to. I'm not hounding a bitch about my nigga."

"Well, this my nigga Harmony, and imma do what I feel like concerning it!"

"Well don't concern us every time your nigga strays," Harmony had attitude behind those words.

"I don't know where the hell the attitude coming from, but I don't need this shit." Capri ended the call but quickly received another one from London. "Hello?" Capri was aggravated.

"Yo Capri, I don't know what the hell was wrong with Harmony just now."

"I don't know either, but I don't have time for the shit. Like what kind of friend is that? She can kiss my ass bruh."

"I don't know. She means well but that was just harsh. Anyways, y'all will get over it as always. What I want to know is, are we driving by this bitch's house?" London was serious. For a white girl, she'd had her fair share of run-ins with black girls, and she wasn't afraid to go to war. She enjoyed it.

"Nah London. Imma chill. Cause I'm telling you. I'm gone end up breaking her face I'm so mad."

"Well call me if you ready!"

"I got you boo," Capri put her phone down and looked at the half put up decorations that filled her living room. Capri was fuming and nothing was going to solve this but seeing Travis's face. She

pulled out her phone to text him to come home. She

was going to get to the bottom of this shit.

Chapter Nine: The fine art of bullshit

Finishing the decorations would've been put to the back burner if Capri didn't need something to preoccupy her mind. Capri felt enraged at the fact that they were just now doing well again, and he couldn't let these females go. Hoes, his baby mama, and now this Brittany chick. However, when he got home, she planned on getting some straightening done.

Capri cleaned up the decorations she didn't plan on using and put them back in the utility closet. She pulled out the little gifts she had bought for Jada and started wrapping them so she would have something underneath her bare tree.

Capri texted her mother to see if they had plans for Christmas. To her surprise, they were planning a romantic getaway and weren't planning to do the family get-together. This made Capri kind of sad because being around her family during the holidays helped cheer her up towards the end of the year. She was the only child so besides her girls, she didn't have anyone to confide in.

After a few hours had passed and she was now lounging on the couch, and Travis was making his way through the door. "What's up, baby!"

Capri counted down in her head trying not to be at an all-time high with her step down she was about to have, but it's like the petty gods had taken over and she was no longer in control. "Don't hey baby me, I thought this bitch Brittany was a bitch your homies were fucking with. All the while you the nigga she is calling daddy. You know what, you make me fucking sick!"

"Capri I just walked through the house. You think I want to deal with this bullshit."

"It's only bullshit cause it's not me. Let me be out here wilding like you do. I'd never hear the end of it. You know what though, have your hoes because baby another nigga would love to have me and only me!" Capri got back comfortable on the couch and closed her eyes.

"The fuck did you just say?" Travis slammed his keys down on the living room table and stood over Capri.

"Travis get the fuck from around me. Go call Brittany or your baby mother and try to run down on them how you are doing me. You want to do your own thing, fine! However, don't stop me when it's my turn."

"You know what Capri that shit ain't even funny!"

"Who's laughing Travis? Seems like to me all your hoes laughing at me thinking I'm a joke cause my nigga can't keep his dick in his pants. Believe me, though, women always better at this shit, so you gone see!"

"Capri I'll kill you and any nigga that dares to push up on you so please stop playing with me. You just saying shit now."

"Yeah okay!" Capri got more comfortable under her blanket.

"Yo I'm not playing with you Capri. Damn what you want a nigga to do. Like damn I be trying but I be getting caught up with this shit. I don't know why I do this shit. I don't be trying to hurt you."

"Welp maybe you should try a lot harder cause all you do is hurt me, Travis. I'm sick of it. I don't have to deal with this. I choose to. But I'm tired of fighting with hoes and your baby mama behind you. I want a man that has ties to me and me only. We have been doing this shit for too long to be still going through *this* shit."

"Listen Capri. I promise I'm going to put forth effort into changing my ways. I'll cut this hoe Brittany off, block her, and all of that. But you are talking about another nigga is just blowing me right now. You know you belong to me and me only."

"Well act like it. Cause it ain't too many more chances I got left in me. I'm tired and I want to be loved correctly." Capri got a little choked up, but she held it in.

Travis came over and kissed Capri on the top of the head. He left out of the room and all she could do was shake her head and let the tears fall quick enough to wipe away before he came back. Did she want to believe that he would change, yes. Did she believe that he could change, no. Travis's actions never lived up to the apology.

Capri thought about her fight with Harmony earlier and wondered and had been her problem lately. Although Harmony had always been like the big sister to the girls, lately it seemed as if they were beneath her. Capri couldn't put her hand on it, but something deep down made her start to question Harmony and her loyalty.

Capri snapped out of her deep thoughts as Travis entered the living room. He sat down on the other end of her. "Here, I want you to see this!"

Travis handed Capri his phone. He had sent a text to Brittany telling her to never text him again and he was done fucking around with her. Capri was slightly satisfied but she knew if it wasn't her, it'll be someone else, sooner or later. "Okay congratulations. Still gone fire off on the hoe if I see her. These bitches don't know their place."

Travis took his phone back and sighed. "Nothing is ever good enough."

"You not cheating is good enough. That would definitely be a start!"

"Damnit I get it Capri can you please drop it?" Travis seemed to be getting aggravated.

"I ain't got shit else to say!"

Travis sat there looking at her. "Listen my mom want us to come over at some point for Christmas. I don't know what the plan was."

"That's fine. My mom and dad are supposed to be going on vacation anyways. So, we not going over there this year."

"Cool. I'll let her know then. Listen, baby, don't be in the slums. We gone get this shit right."

Capri looked at him and although she was thinking *I'd heard all of this before*, she simply answered, "Yeah I know Travis, I know."

Chapter Ten: Expecting the Unexpected

Capri rolled her eyes as she lugged all the gifts and gift bags out of the car. Travis's dad came out of the house and looked at Travis coming up the driveway. "Boy if you don't help that woman with them gifts."

"Dad you know she thinks she's superwoman."

"Grab the damn boxes Travis, have that woman carrying all that stuff." Travis's father demanded.

"Damn pops," Travis stopped right in his tracks and turned around and grabbed the bags from Capri.

"Thank you," she said sarcastically.

"Come here Capri girl, I feel like I haven't seen you in forever." Travis's father Bernard pulled Capri into a hug.

"Yeah, I think the last time we were over here was for Thanksgiving. You know we are steadily working."

"Trust me I know about that. Well, yall come in, take a load off." Bernard opened the front door.

Capri and Bernard always seemed to get along. Since the first time they were introduced, they seemed to hit it off. It was Travis's mother, Alayne that seemed to give Capri the most issues. They always had a nice nasty relationship with each other. Sometimes they didn't like being around each other and some days it was cool.

Capri worried what type of Alayne she would get today but she was prepared for whatever. As they entered the house the smell of good cooking hit her nose. The Christmas spirit filled the house as she noticed all the decorations streamed across the walls and stairs. The Christmas tree was huge and filled with gold and red decorations.

"Is that my baby boy?" Alayne came down from the stairs and embraced her son.

"What's up Ma!"

"Oh, it's so nice to have you and your sister here for Christmas. You know Charmaine just got here from North Carolina, she in the kitchen."

"Oh, she is, let me drop these gifts off and go speak." Travis walked into the living room.

Capri waited a while to see if Travis's mom planned on speaking. When she realized that she wasn't she took the initiative. "Hey, Ms. Alayne!"

"Hey baby," Alayne said dryly.

Capri smirked and walked into the living where it seemed to be the liveliest. Travis's little cousin was running around playing with a foam football. His aunties both were sitting on the couch talking with each other. Capri took a place on the edge of one of the chairs by the Christmas tree.

"Hey, Capri," one of the aunties spoke.

"Hey, how are you doing?"

"Doing good, it's nice seeing you. That husband of yours just dropped this stuff in here and ain't speak to nobody. I'm going to get that boy."

"Yeah, he has a habit of being on a one tract mind sometimes." Capri giggled.

"Capri come here for a second." Travis peeked his head into the living room. Capri's eyes questioned him, but she reluctantly joined him in the hallway they had just left out of.

"Yo, I want to tell you this before some shit pop off, my mom invited Jada and Reign over here."

"The fuck you mean invited her over here?" Capri said through gritted teeth. Obviously, she didn't care about baby Jada, but why in the hell couldn't Reign just drop Jada off.

"Listen I can't control that woman, but it's Christmas and I just want to enjoy you, my family, and my baby, so can you please try to play nice?"

"You're telling me to play nice when your baby mama is the definition of hell on earth?"

"See there you go, not playing nice." Travis chucked but Capri's face frowned more.

"This isn't funny Travis, seriously, I don't want to be around that bitch."

"Capri, seriously, chill!" Travis's voice got deeper, but she didn't care.

As soon as she was about to say something else, Alayne came from the kitchen with the biggest smile on her face. "Are yall still here in this hallway? Go mingle with the family. You know the young folks out back smoking up my yard. Lord, I hope the neighbors don't call the police. The little children and old folks in the living room being drags and us grown folks in the game room."

"Alright momma, we just talking right now, we gone check everyone out."

Alayne's smile dropped a little bit as she looked over to her son and Capri. She wanted to say something else, but she decided against it and walked away to the back of the house. "Your mom hates me." Capri flatly expressed.

"Capri seriously, my mother doesn't hate you. We are not about to be on this shit for the holidays. You know how to just completely turn things around. I'm going outback!" Without another word, Travis turned away from Capri and headed to where his mother said the people his age was.

"You have to be fucking kidding me!" Capri mumbled softly.

"What was that baby?" Bernard came from the hallway bathroom and startled Capri.

"Whew, you scared me, Mr. Jackson."

"What are you doing up here all alone? Go back there with them risk-takers," he laughed. "That's what I call em'."

"I was headed out there, I just had to get my head together first. I guess Reign is coming over with the baby."

Mr. Jackson shook his head like he wanted to say something, but he didn't. "Well, all the young folks are out there. The best advice I can give you is to grab a drink and just enjoy yourself. Don't let the small stuff or petty people get to you."

"I won't Mr. Jackson and I appreciate you looking out for me."

"You know that's what I'm here for. Hopefully, my son makes an honest woman out of you." Mr. Jackson smiled then disappeared into the living room.

Capri reluctantly went outside to join her man and his cousins. She didn't have a clue when Reign would arrive with the baby, but she dug out the cooler and took out a wine cooler and hoped she

could remain on her best behavior.

Chapter Eleven: A lot like Christmas

"Everyone, the baby is here!" Alayne came outside and announced to the cousins as they all were in tune with the music and drinks. As soon as she said that, both Capri and Travis looked over to the backdoor. Capri got off Travis's lap as Reign and the baby came through the back door.

Capri rolled her eyes at everyone gathering around the baby. For some of them, this was their first time seeing Jada in person, so everyone was in awe. Travis grabbed Capri's hand and squeezed it before joining the forming circle and grabbing his baby out of Reign's hand. She stood there smiling while Alayne rubbed her back.

Capri was getting pissed off by the second. She went over to the large coolers and grabbed another drink. If she was going to have to sit through this fake-ass Christmas celebration, she damn sure wasn't going to do it sober. *Didn't Reign have her own damn family to annoy?* Capri thought as she took a huge swig from the glass bottle.

"Take it easy there!" Penelope, one of Travis older cousin suggested.

"Trust me it's either this or turn yall family function into Monday night brawl!"

Penelope laughed, but Capri looked over at Reign with hate in her eyes because she wasn't joking.

"Girl don't even let that shit bother you. My cousin loves you, he's here with you, she's here because she's trying to fit in. We don't even fuck with her like that."

"Yeah, maybe some don't, but your auntie sure does. Probably just to spite me," Capri took another sip.

"Auntie doesn't like nobody for real, she's a bitch, to be honest, but we love her. I'm telling you don't let this shit bother you. Hold your weight remember your position." Penelope squeezed Capri's shoulder and went to join the baby-watching crew.

Capri sat down in the lawn chair and watched as her man showed Jada off. Eventually, everyone returned to what they were doing. Travis made his way over to Capri and she straightened up in the chair. "Baby, will you hold Jada? I need to go holler at her momma."

"The fuck you need to talk to her for?" Capri was confused.

"Man don't start. I'm just making sure she's not here on no bullshit that's it."

"I'd hoped she'd know not to come here with no bullshit unless she wants my foot in her ass!"

"Man, you gone hold Jada or not, I'm not on this shit today."

"Give her here, but don't take long cause that shit ain't even necessary for real." Travis handed Capri the baby and walked off without another word. Capri put her bottle down on the table next to her and stood Jada up on her legs. "Your daddy and your mama keep trying me. I'm going to bust both of them in the head." It was obvious that Jada didn't understand her, but she cooed and smiled in Capri's direction.

Capri watched as Travis grabbed Reign's arm and pulled her into the house. It made her uncomfortable about how he was handling her, but she put it to the back of her head. She noticed Alayne making eye contact with her, and Capri rolled her eyes and focused back on Jada, "your grandmother can get her ass beat too!" Capri said in a baby voice.

Capri started to giggle a little bit and she could tell the effects of the drink started to make her feel good and tipsy. Penelope pulled a chair over to where Capri was sitting. "See what I mean. Know your position."

Capri smiled but, in her head, she was thinking who the hell would want to be in this position. It was embarrassing that a man she'd spent three years of her life with was parading around a baby that didn't come from her. "This ain't no position to brag about." She sat Jada down on her lap.

"I mean, you knew it was going to be something like this when you decided to stay with Travis. Birthdays, Christmas, Thanksgiving, hell any type of celebration Reign is going to try to throw that baby mama weight around."

"Yeah, that's the shit I don't have time for. She's only here because she hasn't moved on. Why else would she be here?"

"I mean you might be right, but this is your shit, don't let her being here get you out of character."

"With all due respect Penelope, I don't even want to be talking about her, celebrations, or who holds the most weight contest right now. I'm simply trying to get through this day."

Penelope nodded her head and remained silent about the topic. "She's a cutie, looks just like her father."

"Yeah, that's what I said. She keeps us on our toes."

The back door opened, and Reign came out looking irritated. Alayne walked up to her, and her face seemed to change. At the same time, both Alayne and Reign looked over at Capri. Capri grabbed her bottle off the table and took another drink until the light pink liquid was gone. She damn near slammed the bottle on the table causing even Jada to jump.

She turned Jada around and started to talk gibberish to her so that she wouldn't bust out into tears.

"You're good at this. Looks fitting." Penelope smiled at Capri. "Are you two thinking about babies?"

"Oh no, definitely not. I can't see myself with two under two. Hell, when we have Jada it's more like I have Jada and I'm not about to put that extra stress on me. Plus, we have plenty of other things to worry about than bringing a child into this."

Reign and Alayne were making their way over to Where Capri and Penelope were sitting. "Keep your cool ma," Penelope warned before the duo got close.

"Nah, she better!"

"What's up Capri?" Reign greeted Capri as if they were friends or something. She knew she was putting on an act for Alayne because the hoe knew not to speak to her. Especially right now. Capri sat there slightly bouncing Jada with a blank expression on her face. Reign turned to Penelope, "What's up P!"

"What's up Reign, how are you?"

"I'm good. Such a nice day out. This is your first-time meeting Jada huh?" Reign questioned.

"Sure is. Auntie sent me pictures, but it didn't do any justice. She's a cutie."

"Thank you, people say she looks like me, her *mama,* but everyone here seems to think she looks just like daddy," Reign smirked.

Capri wanted to punch her in the throat in that very instant, but she held in and attempted to keep her cool.

"That baby looks like me, sorry to tell y'all!" Alayne laughed and rubbed Reign's back. To Capri, it seemed like Mrs. Jackson was doing the most trying to be extra friendly with Reign, but she didn't care. If she knew how Reign was outside of her property it would be a whole different story. Or hell maybe it wouldn't be, the type of chick Travis's mother seemed to be the more Capri was around her, Reign and Alayne were a perfect match.

"Auntie come here!" Someone screamed from across the yard.

"I'll be right back babies." The girls watched as Alayne walked to see what the commotion was about.

As soon as she was out of ear's reach, Reign's head swiveled in Capri's direction. "What's up stepmama you can't speak?"

"Reign, why the fuck are you trying me? I don't fuck with you. Why are you talking to me?"

Reign chuckled and shifted her weight. "Baby daddy told me to play nice. I'm just trying to do what I was told."

"Okay, well play nice the fuck up outta my face, before we have an issue!"

"What issue might that be?" Reign challenged.

"Whoa ladies, the baby is right here, besides we are at my auntie's house and we're all here for a reason. Let's not do this!" Penelope sat on the edge of the chair.

"No P, I'm just trying to see what issues we might have from miss thing here?" Reign smiled devilishly.

"I don't know maybe you getting your ass beat, for like what, the fifth time now. Please get the fuck out my face."

"Girl please I'm not worried about a fuck thing happening to me. Hand me my baby bitch."

"Gladly, HOE!" Capri stood up and handed Jada to Reign.

Reign laughed at Capri and grabbed the baby. "Come on Jada let's find daddy." Reign walked over to where Alayne was, and Capri got out of her chair and into the house to find Travis.

As she walked through the hallway she bumped right into Charmaine. "What's up, sis!" Charmaine was a lot more friendly than her mom and since Capri and Travis had been dating, she was always nice to Capri.

"Hey hun, you seen your brother?"

"I did a little while ago. Him and that ratchet baby mama of his. I haven't seen him recently though."

"Well, when you see him can you tell him I took a walk. I need to get some air."

"Alright, sis I got you!"

Capri quietly made her way out the front door and down the neighborhood sidewalk. She was over this fake family bullshit.

Chapter Twelve: Someone Like You

Capri started her walk down the sidewalk going nowhere in particular. Capri was trying to figure out how she'd gotten in this situation. How could she have stayed through all this shit she'd been put through. Capri's phone started to ring, and she decided against answering it. She knew it was Travis but right now she just wanted to be alone.

As she walked down the sidewalk, she spotted a couple getting out of the car. The man came around to the back seat and opened the door for his woman. She got out of the car in a nice fitting sleep gown. Capri could tell that she had just had a baby. She then pulled the tiniest baby from the car and her man reached out and kissed her on the head. Closing the door behind her, they both walked into the entrance of their home and Capri started to cry.

She thought about how that would never be her life if she continued down her path. Hell, her man already had a baby so it wouldn't be so special if she popped out with one. She'd always be interwoven with the mess that Travis and his baby mama kept up and to make matters worse there was always some new hoe she had to deal with and put in their place.

True and true she was tired, and she knew she deserved more than what was given out to her. Capri just was so hurt that Travis couldn't see that he'd hurt her in ways unimaginable. He'd completely broken her down and a day like this, when it's supposed to feel jolly and in good spirits, she was yet having to be reminded of his fuck ups.

Every time she had to do something for Jada, or he had to leave and go check on Jada or even when Reign decided to pop by their house was just a consistent reminder of the betrayal. Capri's phone started to ring in her pocket again. As she pulled it out, she saw Travis's name flashing across the phone. Reluctantly she answered, "hello?"

"Capri where are you man?" Travis sounded annoyed.

"Listen, Travis, I needed some air. Your baby mama on that goofy shit and I'm trying to respect your parent's home, so I'm walking right now."

"Capri are you serious. Like damn it's not a big deal. I talked to her, and she knows to stay clear."

"You say that, yet the bitch come up to me being funny as a muthafucka trying to push the baby mama shit around in my face."

"Capri bruh you are doing all this on Christmas?"

"I ain't doing shit! Ask Penelope, she was right there when ya baby mama was popping off. I should've just hit that bitch. Your mom's wild disrespectful to me and you let her be! I'm sick of all this shit!"

"Well, if you are so sick, why are you still with me?"

Capri looked at her phone shocked as hell, not even believing the fact that he would ask her that silly-ass question, "well if you don't know, then I don't either. Goodbye Travis."

Capri hung up the phone and it instantly started ringing again. She placed the phone back in her pocket and continued her walk until she saw a park. Capri spotted the park bench and decided to take a load of. It was quiet out. Not many cars passed by her, and she somehow felt at peace. She thought about just getting an Uber and taking herself back home but then she would be lonely.

London was out of town, and she didn't want to bother her with drama on Christmas. Even though they had spoken since they got into a heated argument, Harmony was still acting bitchy from the conversation they had. So, Capri wasn't about to reach out to her about this. It would've just added more fuel to their friendship fire she was trying so hard to extinguish.

As she pulled her phone out a grey Pitbull came running up to her, jumping on her lap causing her to drop it. "Ah, what the fuck!" Capri screamed running behind the park bench.

"Lola bring your ass here," a man in some jogging attire ran up grabbing the leash that was dangling behind the dog. "Ma'am I'm so sorry about that!"

"I would say put that big ass dog on a leash but that seems not to be the problem." Capri had her hand over her chest. She wasn't afraid of dogs but an unwarranted approach by one had her shook.

"Yeah, she got away from me. My bad shorty. She's friendly as you can tell." The man flashed a sly smile. He was a tall, clear cut, chocolate brother with very precise features. His muscular frame was known from the tight-fitting breathable tracksuit. Capri thought he looked like the type to stare at his reflection before leaving out the door.

"It's all good. Just startled me. That's all."

He pulled the dog closer to him. "Why you out here all alone on Christmas Day?" He picked up her phone and handed it to her.

"Ah, I needed some fresh air. A little bit of family drama." Capri giggled nervously.

"That can't be too good. Not good to be out here alone getting attacked by dogs," he joked.

"Righhht," Capri matched his sarcasm.

"Again, sorry about that. I was taking Lola for a run, apparently, I wasn't running fast enough."

"Yeah, I see." Capri sat back down on the bench and checked her phone for any scratches.

"So, are you out here alone?" The man looked at her funny.

Capri looked around then looked at him funny as well, "I'm the only person you see right?"

"Nah I mean like out here in this neighborhood. I've never seen you around, so I assumed you were visiting. I didn't catch your name."

"Oh, yeah, I'm here with my boyfriend and his family. The Jacksons. My name is Capri."

"Oh, okay, Carpi, well I am Alonzo, but I know that family. Nice people, well except for that mother. She's a little high maintenance. No disrespect or anything." The man said quickly.

"Oh no, I don't like the bitch!" Lola came close to Capri, and she patted her on the head.

The man couldn't help but let his laughter escape. "Wow, like that huh?"

"Yeah, you know how some people are just difficult for no reason? Well, that would be Mrs. Jackson, just a bitch for no reason at all."

"Well sorry to hear that, I don't have that issue currently, but I can only imagine the drama for days like this."

"Yup that's exactly why I'm here and they are there." Just as she said that she noticed that Travis was walking up to them. She was still irritated with him, and her face instantly turned upside down. Alonzo could tell that she was looking at something behind her and turned around.

Lola instantly started barking and trying to get closer to Travis. Travis stopped walking towards the two and called over, "Ayo, Capri, what the hell man, you don't see me calling you?"

"I guess I'll see you around maybe." Alonzo kept tugging on Lola as much as he could.

Capri lifted off the park bench and patted Lola once more before walking in Travis's direction.

"The way today is going I don't know if I will be in this neighborhood any time soon." Capri laughed.

"Yo Capri, what the fuck?" Travis had a mug on his face now and Capri rolled her eyes and walked in his direction. Travis watched as the man and dog walked in the opposite direction as them. "Who in the hell was that you were talking to?"

"Hell, if I know, some dude walking his dog. I told you I was going out for air. Why did you come looking for me?"

"Well, I got concerned that you were walking around by yourself on Christmas day, but it seems like you were occupied." Capri could sense his jealousness in the air.

"What the fuck ever, I know you of all people aren't trying to insinuate what you are trying to when you have a whole baby mama at the family Christmas get-together, this is why I needed some air. I just can't with you right now."

Capri watched as Lola and her owner Alonzo jogged away. She imagined herself jogging alongside them. It was better than what she was about to walk into.

Chapter Thirteen: Our Last Chance

Capri and Travis walked through the door and most of the family were entering the living room. Reign was bouncing the baby on her leg. Reign spotted the couple coming through the door and she rolled her eyes at the two.

"Okay family, I want everyone to settle down. We finally found Capri so now we can begin." Mrs. Jackson said very condescendingly. "Now we are about to open some gifts, but before we get started, I just want to say how blessed I am to see all my family here today. Year after year we continue to push through this family tradition. I just want to say to my husband I love you with all of my heart, my children, I am so blessed that you both grew up to be stand-up adults." Everyone was in awe as Mrs. Jackson spoke, but Capri could gag at any moment. "And to Reign, you are just as well as part of this family than anyone. I am so blessed to have you and my first grandchild here with us. I am so glad that I get to see baby Jada grow up with two lovely parents." At this point the room was so quiet you could hear a cotton ball drop.

Capri looked out towards the family members that were looking at her. Travis was looking at his mother like she had lost his mind and Mr. Jackson was pulling his wife closer. "I think what my lady is trying to say is that we are so blessed to have all the family around us on this wonderful holiday."

"I think my choice of words was good honey. Anyways, I want everyone to go and look under the tree and find a gift with their name on it. On the count of three, we are all going to open the first gift together, and then afterward you all can just open whatever. Reign baby, there is something under there from me to you and the baby. I hope you enjoy it."

"That's it, Travis, I can't take this fake ass shit anymore. I am ready to go home and if you don't want to take me home, I will catch a ride my damn self." Capri whispered to Travis.

"Just chill Capri." Travis stood in front of the room and attempted to get everyone's attention. The room was so focused on getting their present from under the tree, hoping for something good, that they didn't even notice Travis's voice. "Excuse me, family, I have an announcement to make!"

"Boy can't it wait until we open our gifts," Penelope said while she was digging under the tree.

"Boy what you trying to say?" Mrs. Jackson said annoyed. Capri was a few seconds from telling her how she felt.

"Okay family please can I have your attention!" Travis spoke louder this time. The family finished grabbing their last items and all returned to the spots they were sitting in. "Okay, I just want to piggyback on what my mother and father were saying and say how grateful I am to be able to spend each holiday with my loved ones. Capri, I'm so glad that each year you can spend the time with my family and me." As Travis said that Mrs. Jackson coughed quietly, but loud enough to cause a disruption. Reign could be heard chuckling in the background. As soon as Capri was about to open her mouth, Travis started to speak again. "Capri, 3 years ago you came into my life, and you captured my love by being exactly who you are till this day. You are the sweetest, most loving, compassionate person I have ever known. Even throughout all my mistakes, you have decided to stick with a nigga, and you have been my very best friend through it all. You are even a wonderful person to my daughter who I love so much. I just want to use this time to ask you a very important question."

Awes and oohs filled the room for some, however, both Mrs. Jackson and Reign moved closer to Travis. "Travis, I know you are not about to propose!" Mrs. Jackson was flushed red.

"Alayne get out of them children's business!" Mr. Jackson pulled Alayne close to him.

"Capri, will you marry me?" Travis ignored the obvious signs of disruption and attempted to complete his proposal.

"Oh, so this what we doing Travis? You just gone be face first in my pussy a couple of nights ago and now you want to play the perfect man to this bitch. That's the shit I be talking about. You are wanting to be all family man when you be over my house to "see Jada", but then want to get up in here and propose to this bitch."

Charmaine jumped up out of her seat and got closer to Reign. "You should watch your mouth at my parent's house. I don't know what yall got going on, but you see my brother is in the middle of doing some shit and you trying to play homewrecker like you're good at."

As all this was going on no one could see the tears started to well up in Capri's eyes. Her breathing had started to heave, and she felt as if she was going to pass out.

"Who told you that it was okay to propose on Christmas day in my house?" Alayne placed her hands on her hips.

"Let the damn boy get his proposal out, yall can mess up a wet dream," one of the aunties yelled out loud.

"Nah, I'm just trying to figure out how my family man is all ready to be a husband now!" Reign said sarcastically.

"Bitch, I'm seconds from fucking you up. You on that funny shit," Charmaine was now in Reign's face.

"Would everyone please just shut the fuck up!" Travis screamed to the top of his lungs. The whole room got quiet, even the kids who had already opened and started to play with their first presents.

"Capri, as I was trying to say, will you please do me the honor of being my wife?"

"This some bullshit!" Reign sat down with the baby and started mumbling things under her breath. The family kind of got away from the attention Travis once had and started doing their own thing.

"Capri?" Travis asked nervously. He pulled out a ring box from his back pocket and opened it. Capri couldn't lie, it was beautiful, but her mind was already on something else.

"Travis I can't do this," Capri said lowly. The family then got quiet.

"What you say, baby?" Travis slightly stood up.

"I said I can't do this. Look at this, look how unperfect this is. This is supposed to be one of the happiest days in my life and it's just ruined, from your baby mama to your ridiculous ass mother. This shit is not right."

"What did you just say?" both Reign and Alayne said at the same time.

"Yall heard what the fuck I said. Fuck this and fuck yall!" Capri started to walk out the front door. Travis was right on her heels.

"Travis, I know you not chasing that disrespectful broad out this house."

Capri stopped dead in her tracks causing Travis to bump into her, "Let me tell you something Mrs. Jackson, I've let you say what you wanted to say over these three years, I let you disrespect me in ways my mother wouldn't even dare to, but let me tell you something bitch, if you ever disrespect me again, I will beat the fuck out you!"

"Now wait a damn minute," Charmaine jumped up to defend her mother.

"I don't care you all sit around and let this woman just disrespect me because she thinks she can, but I'd never marry into a family like this and to a cheating ass nigga like you Travis. Now get the fuck out my face while I leave this motherfucker. Travis, it's over!"

Chapter Fourteen: Empty Words

Capri stormed inside of her home after getting out of the Uber she managed to wrangle up while Travis sat there begging and pleading with her to reconsider all the words she had just said. However, Capri had been through enough, from the lying to the cheating, from Travis's fucked up family. This Christmas was beginning to feel like hell, and she wanted no parts, this day or ever.

Thinking about the allegations that Reign threw out in the middle of Travis's proposal made Capri sick to her stomach. As much as she knew that Reign would say just about anything to get up under her skin, Capri knew that she had to be telling the truth. Why lie about something like that?

Capri went to the kitchen and grabbed trash bags and entered the room that she and Travis once shared. She thought back to what Harmony had told her, *"Only you know when you've had enough,"* and truly today was her enough.

She used all the strength she had in her and pile by pile she grabbed all of Travis's clothes and threw them in trash bags until they were too heavy for her to lift. As soon as she got one bag full, she lugged it to the front door, turning around and filling up a new bag. From his clothes to his shoes, and all the expendables he had lying around the house, everything went in trash bags and plastic tubs that she could find.

Capri was gaining control back for her life.

As much as she wanted to blame herself for how out

of control this situation had become it was no one's

fault but Travis. He decided to step out on her, he

decided to creep and create a child out of their

commitment that she thought they shared.

She thought back to all the times that Travis

had ever said he was sorry for constantly messing up

and questioned herself if he ever really meant it. She

wondered if she caused her demise. She told him

countless times about how she wanted and expected

to be treated. It's like he only heard this and done the

complete opposite.

Capri wondered if he trained his mind on

what he could do to her based on what she always

forgave him for. Hell, if she forgave him countless

times, why would he stop and think, maybe I

shouldn't cheat anymore. Capri got so enraged both tears and snot started to pour down her face. She grabbed anything she could get her hands on and started to throw it across the room. Everything that stood in her way became something that she flung against the wall.

So much anger filled her heart, and she was glad that Travis decided not to follow her because there was no telling what she might do to him. Trying to request a lifestyle change for a man who didn't want to see a change within himself was now dead to Capri. She vowed on this day that she would no longer beg for a man to love her the way she knew she should be loved.

The right man would love her without the lies, without the cheating, and without the heartbreak. Capri collapsed in the middle of her floor and cried until she felt puffy in the face. She knew that she had to set this boundary. If not, she would always be in a cat and mouse game with some hoe Travis decided to screw, even down to his baby mama. For an hour Capri just sat there and reflected on her life with Travis.

Yes, she could admit that they had some great times together, but the hurt outweighed the good. Just then Capri started hearing shuffling around and some cussing. She got up off the floor and wiped her face. As she stepped out into the hallway and her Travis locked eyes. "Baby?" Travis questioned.

"Travis, please, I don't want to continue to do this. I meant what I said. I don't want to do this anymore. It's too much."

"Baby, please just tell me what I have to do. I will do anything, just let me know."

"Travis there's nothing you can do. All this time it's been a continuation of the deceit and the bullshit. Every time I have to look at Jada it's a constant reminder of what you have done to me. And I just can't take it. This time I'm serious, I'm done."

"Capri, I want to marry you, I want to finally change my ways and get myself together. I need your help with this. I know I fucked up but baby, I'll change. I need you. I am in love with you."

Capri shook her head, "I was in love with your lies Travis. But I don't love you."

"How could you say some shit like that?"

"Just how I did. Please just leave, don't make this harder than it needs to be. I just, please," Capri started to walk back into the room and Travis stood there dumbfounded.

For a little while, Capri could hear the door opening and closing and she figured Travis was loading his things into his car. Capri always gave second, third chances but something in her let her know that this was it. She would no longer settle for less when she knew she was worth so much more.

She felt wiser and she vowed to herself, when she was able to repair from this heartbreak, she'd never allowed herself to beg for love, lie for love, or be dumb for love. Capri would never again fall in love with lies.

The End.

<u>Books from The Author</u>

Always At Your Side

Cleaning Up My Heart: One Bad Boy At A Time

Cleaning Up My Heart Again

Cleaning Up My Heart For The Last Time

Colder Side Of The Pillow

Follow On:

Instagram
- Kaaymac
- Dantwoinykuetheauthor

Facebook
- Kaay Mac
- Authoress Dantwoinykue

Amazon Link: http://tiny.cc/r7siuz